CLAIMING TINY

Charon MC
Book 4

KHLOE WREN

Books by Khloe Wren

Charon MC:
Inking Eagle
Fighting Mac
Chasing Taz
Claiming Tiny
Saving Scout

Fire and Snow:
Guardian's Heart
Noble Guardian
Guardian's Shadow
Fierce Guardian
Necessary Alpha
Protective Instincts

Dragon Warriors:
Enchanting Eilagh
Binding Becky
Claiming Carina
Seducing Skye
Believing Binda

Jaguar Secrets:
Jaguar Secrets
FireStarter

Other Titles:
Fireworks
Tigers Are Forever
Bad Alpha Anthology
Scarred Perfection
Scandals: Zeck
Mirror Image Seduction
Deception
Kings of Sydney: Daniil

ISBN: 978-0-9876275-8-2
Copyright © Khloe Wren 2018

Cover Credits:
Model: Deposit Photo edited by Claudia Bost
Digital Artist: Khloe Wren

Editing Credits:
Editor: Carolyn Depew of Write Right

Biography

Khloe Wren grew up in the Adelaide Hills before her parents moved the family to country South Australia when she was a teen. A few years later, Khloe moved to Melbourne which was where she got her first taste of big city living.

After a few years living in the big city, she missed the fresh air and space of country living so returned to rural South Australia. Khloe currently lives in the Murraylands with her incredibly patient husband, two strong willed young daughters, an energetic dog and two curious cats.

As a child Khloe often had temporary tattoos all over her arms. When she got her first job at 19, she was at the local tattooist in the blink of an eye to get her first real tattoo. Khloe now has four, two taking up much of her back.

While Khloe doesn't ride a bike herself, she loves riding pillion behind her husband on the rare occasion they get to go out without their daughters.

Charon:

Char·on \ˈsher-ən, ˈker-ən, -än\

In Greek mythology, the Charon is the ferryman who takes the dead across either the river Styx or Acheron, depending on whether the soul's destination is the Elysian Fields or Hades.

Prologue

May 2017
Missy

Of all the times I'd thought about my future, this was never something I'd considered. Being a club whore to a motorcycle club wasn't exactly something a woman aspires to. But life is full of unexpected turns and to survive, I was being forced to some extreme lengths. One such turn had led me to where I currently found myself in Bridgewater, Texas, sitting in the office of Scout, the president of the Charon MC, seeking permission to join the club's whore room. When I'd first come up with this idea, I'd figured getting in would be easy, that no one would ask questions before putting me to work.

I couldn't have been more wrong.

Scout was full of questions, and I had no clue if I could trust him. So far I'd avoided answering anything other than my name and age, but that wasn't going to last.

"Sweetheart, don't look so scared. No one here is gonna hurt you. But I need to know if you've got shit following you that we're gonna have to deal with. Any information you give me ain't gonna leave this room."

Tears pricked my eyes as the man before me just transformed from gruff biker to concerned father-figure. I had no idea who my biological father was, and my stepfather wasn't worth the air he breathed. He'd certainly never spoken to me like Scout just had. The friendly tone loosened my lips before my mind knew what was happening.

"I don't know if they'll try to look for me."

"Who are *they*, darlin'?"

Nerves had me biting my lower lip for a moment.

"My stepfather and his family. You see, my mother, she died and, ah, since I don't like my stepfamily much, I left."

I might be talking, but I didn't want to say too much. Not until I saw what he would do with the little bit of information I gave him. It didn't help me gauge his reaction, when his expression stayed carefully blank, but I got the sense there were a whole heap going on beneath it. That he wasn't unaffected by my words.

"Where did you live?"

"Soule. It's north-west from here, nothing but a speck on the map in the middle of Texas, really."

"That where your stepfamily still is?"

I gave him a nod as I wiped my palms on my thighs. He was going to grill me until he knew it all. I shot a quick glance at the closed door. I should leave, keep running.

"As far as I know."

Maybe this was all a huge mistake.

When I fled Soule, I'd been desperate and risked hitchhiking to get far away from there. The trucker who'd stopped for me was on his way to Houston. He'd made me the offer that if I didn't mind taking care of him on the road, he'd take me all the way with him. I'd done worse for less, so I'd agreed.

As we'd travelled, he'd told me about a motorcycle club near where he grew up. The Charon MC had a reputation of taking care of everyone in their town, Bridgewater, Texas, and for keeping drugs and trouble out of it. Apparently, this club also kept a number of women around the clubhouse for the sole purpose of looking after the club's sexual needs. He'd assured me the club looked after its whores well, even providing housing if they required it. He'd also told me he'd never heard any rumors of any of the women in the club being mistreated. By the time we'd reached Houston, he'd had me convinced it would be a good next step for me. And after I'd agreed to spend the night in his bed, he'd given me the money I needed for the bus fare to get from Houston to Bridgewater.

Scout stood from behind the desk and I stiffened when he sat next to me on the couch. Was he about to tell me to get the hell out? Sitting at an angle, he caught and held my gaze with his.

"Mercedes, I can keep asking you questions all damn day, or you can save us both some time, and a lot of bullshit, and be fucking straight with me. What are you running from?"

I searched his gaze and expression, weighing my options. But really, what options did I have? Either I put my trust in Scout and the Charon MC, or I left and kept running. Closing my eyes, I took a deep breath. I had no money, and I knew I'd gotten lucky with that trucker. Next time, I could end up dead.

Since leaving the commune, I'd come to realize just how little I knew about the outside world, and how to survive in it. But with my mother gone, I literally had nowhere to go. So, I decided to put my life in the hands of the Charons and tell Scout everything.

"I was born in Mexico. My mother snuck across the border with me when I was a toddler. I have no idea what she was running from, she never told me. And I don't remember much about those early years, just the odd flash of memory here and there. Somehow, we ended up at this commune in Soule, Texas. I guess she figured it was remote enough we'd be safe from whatever it was that sent her running in the first place. Or maybe my step-father found us and took us there."

I shrugged, because in truth, I wasn't sure about a lot of things.

"It wasn't long before Mama ended up marrying one of the elders of the commune. That was right about the time she started sending me to school."

I had a feeling that the commune's idea of school wasn't anything like the ones the outside world had, so I didn't give Scout any details. He didn't need to know what I was taught there to understand who might come looking for me.

"The school days were long, then when I was old enough, I moved from school to work, which also meant long days. It also meant I moved into the bunkhouse with the other unmarried women. So I had no idea what was happening. I barely saw Mama, let alone what she was being put through."

Tears pricked my eyes. Maybe if I'd fought harder I could have stayed living at home, and would have seen what was going on. Found some way to get both of us out of there before it was too late.

"The commune had this big kitchen were most of us ate all our meals. I worked there, washing dishes mainly, but I also did a little of the cooking. Yesterday, while we were cleaning up after breakfast, another of the girls told me she'd seen my stepfather at breakfast, but not my mother. We were both worried something had happened, so she helped me slip out the back and I ran to my stepfather's house."

Dashing the tears from my face, I stopped talking as I tried to get my emotions under control.

"What'd you find, sugar?"

The image of how I'd found my mother filled my sight. Her naked body had been a mass of old and new bruises, and so much blood. And the pain etched on her face was something I'd never get out of my head. I couldn't bring myself to speak about how she used her last breaths to tell me to run. To warn me what would happen if I stayed, and that it wasn't worth the risk to go back and get any of my belongings before I left. I couldn't admit to Scout how I'd been a coward and ran. How I'd left my mother behind, without even attempting to get her medical help.

I cleared my throat.

"I found her dead, then I ran."

"Tell me what happened to your mother."

The growl in his tone told me he'd already worked it out. Did I really have to say it?

"You can guess. I can't—I'm not ready to go into it."

"Yeah, I can. I can also understand not wanting to talk about it, but I need you to. At least a little. I gotta understand what the fuck is going on with you before I can let you stay. And I'm also guessing she wasn't dead when you found her. Because if she was, you'd have called whatever that commune had in the way of law enforcement, or medical help to try to revive her, but you didn't. You fled. Why?"

My shoulders slumped and I let my head drop down. "I watched her take her last breath before I left. She told me that my stepfather had given his blessing to another of the elders to claim me for his own now that they were finished with her." I looked up and locked my stare with Scout's. "I swear I had no idea what had been going on."

Nope, I'd not had a clue that my own mother was using her body to pay for my freedom. A shiver ran up my spine and I dropped my gaze away again.

"I was so naive. So stupid. Even after having spent just a little time outside of that place I can see how fucked up it was. The women, both as children and adults, were little more than slaves—"

"Mercedes, none of what happened was your fault. You were raised there, you didn't know anything better. I'm actually a little amazed you ran and got out like you did."

"Mama didn't waste words telling me what my life would be like if I stayed. And I saw her, saw what those animals had done to her."

I was now trembling with rage and grief. So much so I was struggling to speak through it. Up until now, I'd been focused solely on getting as far away from the commune as possible. I hadn't given myself time to really process what had happened that day.

"Well, you did the right thing in leaving that place. However, I am curious about how you ended up on our doorstep. How'd you hear about the Charon MC?"

"I ran south until I found a highway. Then, wanting to get away as fast as possible, I risked hitching. A trucker picked me up. He, ah, he grew up around here and was on a run to Houston, and on the drive we chatted and he told me about the Charon MC, that you keep your town safe and have women you keep here at the clubhouse." I shrugged. "I had nowhere else to go. I've got no family or friends I can call on. Your club seemed as good a place as any to land."

He nodded and adjusted the bandana wrapped around

his head. He seemed to do that a lot. "Okay. So, in the last twenty-four hours have you seen any signs of them following you?"

I shook my head. "No one saw me leave. The other girl in the kitchen only knew I was going to check on my mother, and she wouldn't rat me out. She'd get in a lot of trouble if she admitted to knowing anything about my disappearance. So, I've got no idea how long it took my stepfather to realize I was gone. I haven't seen anyone who looks familiar at all as I travelled."

Scout's gaze turned more serious. "If you do, if you see or hear anything that makes you think they've found you? You need to come tell me, or any of the other Charons. We will keep you safe, Mercedes. Now, about what you came here for. You sure you want to join the whores? We could probably work out something for you elsewhere, work-wise. Maybe waitressing at a cafe, or bar."

Sucking back the last of my emotions and locking them away, I gave him a small smile. "Is that your polite way of asking if I have any experience? I didn't think bikers were that polite."

He shook his head at me with a smirk. "Well, yeah, I was trying to be nice about it. But my men can be rough on a woman, and if you come in here as a club whore, pretty as you are, you'll be used often and well. You prepared for that?"

Not wanting to go into why I was well trained for the job of a club whore, I skated the truth the best I could.

"I know I'm not ready to function out in the world. The commune hasn't given me the knowledge I need to work out in the public. What if someone who knows my stepfather came in and noticed me because I was acting strangely? It's too risky. Something that keeps me out of sight is perfect. And don't worry, I'm not as innocent as you apparently think I am. How do you think I paid for my ride here?" Determined to not give Scout time to ask the questions I could see he wanted to, I pushed ahead. "So, when can I start?"

He frowned for a moment, as though he was going to still ask his questions, but then he simply shook his head and his expression cleared.

"Right now, if you want. Later we'll go over everything else you need to know, and I'll show you to the room you'll spend most of your time in when you're here at the clubhouse. You can live in with a few of the other girls. We have a house close by where some of the whores live. The others will tell you how things work. You need to know the most important rules before we do anything, though. Don't fuck with the old ladies. You don't get to pick and choose who you wanna fuck—a brother wants you and you're able—you're his. Don't lose your heart to any of these men, you're not an old lady in waiting, you're a whore here to help my brothers scratch an itch. And you don't leave that room until after ten pm. If any of us see you outside that room while there are still kids running around the place, there will be hell to pay. Understand?"

I nodded.

"One more thing. You're gonna need a different name to use. You want to stay hidden from the world, we're gonna need to call you something other than Mercedes."

With no idea what to call myself, I sat there in silence until he filled it again.

"How about Missy?"

That made me smile. At only five feet three, I knew I was short and it made me look younger than my twenty-one years.

"Sure, why not?"

He smiled at me with a suddenly very heated look that had nothing fatherly about it. *Thankfully.*

"Well, how about you getcha ass over here and show me your skills then, Missy?"

Hoping like hell I hadn't misjudged Scout or the club, I plastered on a smile and with a smooth slide, I shifted closer to him and began my new life as a Charon MC club whore.

Chapter 1

November 2017

Tiny

With another run successfully completed, I was more than ready for a little R&R. Since we were hosting a bunch of the brothers from Satan's Cowboys for the weekend, the clubhouse was hopping when I rode in at a little before ten with the others who'd joined me on the run. Nitro, the Charon's sergeant in arms, had been in charge, so he went straight for Scout's office to do his thing while the rest of us headed out to the bonfire, via the bar to grab a drink.

When I hesitated as I passed the whore room, Keg started chuckling behind me.

"Just go and get your girl already."

A growl rumbled up my throat and I spun to storm the rest of the way down the hallway, unfortunately, with Keg on my heels the whole way.

"She ain't my girl."

My younger club brother scoffed. "You can lie to yourself all you want, brother. The rest of us see the way you two look at each other. Tell me, have you noticed how she's always available when you go looking?"

"She's a club whore, Keg. It's kinda her job to always be fucking available."

And didn't that very thought set my teeth on edge. *Dammit.*

"And that look on your face right now, would be the reason why the prettiest girl in that room is the one used the least."

Clenching the hand not holding my beer into a fist I spun on my brother. "You got no fucking idea what you're talking about."

He shook his head with a sad expression. "Whatever, Tiny. Your loss. Because with the amount of Cowboys here tonight, she won't be left alone for long. Your choice whether you fucking man up and get to her first or not. Despite the rule against it, you wouldn't be the first Charon to pick his old lady from the club whores, you know?"

Knowing that punching Keg wouldn't do anything but prove his point, I took a deep drink from my beer and shoved out the back door and into the shadows of the rear yard. I made the rounds and greeted several of my brothers and a few of the Cowboys who were hanging around before I settled on a log seat toward the rear of the yard. After Keg's little lecture, I wasn't feeling overly fucking sociable. Maybe I should've just headed straight up to my room.

Keg had been right about her looks. Missy was

fucking gorgeous. She obviously had some Mexican blood, with her silky smooth, caramel skin-tone that made my fingers twitch, and that sweet accent of hers. It wasn't strong, and her English was flawless, so I guessed she'd grown up in the US. But fuck me, I only needed to hear her say a word or two before my cock was hard and throbbing for her.

Taking another pull on my beer, I tried to push aside what Keg's words had made me think about, but it was useless. My mind was on that track now. But fuck, old ladies were nothing but trouble. I didn't want, or need one. As I took another mouthful, I glanced around the yard, noticing a few of the brothers whose old ladies hadn't left yet. Keys, the club's secretary and tech expert, had his woman, Donna, up against the fence. Despite the fact the pair of them were in their fifties, Keys, the dirty bugger, had one hand down her pants, while the other was holding her shirt down so her bare tit was out and in his face. Donna had her head back and her fingers tangled in her man's hair. Seeing them had me wondering if maybe having an old lady wasn't so bad.

I turned and caught sight of Bank, another of the men who had a permanent woman. With a wince, I took another drink and looked away from the tense situation that reminded me way too much of my foster home. My foster mother had taught me well that when a woman was that mad, you'd best leave her the fuck alone. I didn't even want to risk eye contact with that one. No idea what the fuck Bank had done, but clearly he was firmly in the doghouse. Memories of the fights between my foster parents flickered through my mind. Drunken father that would storm out and not return for days, equally drunken, drugged-up mother passing out on the couch leaving me, and the other unfortunate kids in their care, to fend for ourselves. Yep, now I remembered why I didn't want an old lady. Didn't want the drama of it all.

As I took my last mouthful of beer, the whores started coming out the back door. Must've ticked past ten pm. Naturally, Missy was among them. The fire light catching on her long shiny black hair as she moved. Why couldn't she have chosen to go into the main bar area inside, where I at least didn't have to see her getting fucked? Keg's words played through my head, that if I just manned up and claimed her, I wouldn't have this fucked-up problem. But I couldn't just fuck her anymore. That last time had pushed me to the edge of my control and I'd nearly fucking claimed her afterwards. Now, a full week later, I was still on edge. Especially when one of the Cowboys pulled Missy up against him. Thankfully, that was when another of the whores came up to me with a couple bottles hanging from her fingers.

"Need a refill, sugar?"

"Sure, babe."

She handed me one of the already-open bottles while she took a mouthful from the other. After taking my first swig, I pulled her to stand between my spread thighs. I had no idea what her name was, and didn't really care. Without me saying a word she slid to her knees, and after she set her bottle on the seat beside us, her long, manicured fingers went for my belt and fly. I kept drinking as she freed my cock and wrapped her glossy lips around me. I groaned as she deep throated me on her first fucking slide down. Damn.

Wrapping my free hand in her blonde curls, my gaze flicked up over her head and suddenly it wasn't Blondie that was sucking my dick. Nope, it was Missy, even though she was actually sucking off a Cowboy across the yard from me. A second Cowboy came up behind Missy, and kneeling down behind her, flipped up her skirt and palmed her bare ass cheeks. With a groan, I fucked up harder into Blondie's mouth, wishing I was across the way, about to slip my cock into Missy's tight little pussy.

The guy at her mouth pulled free and dropped to his knees in front of her. He pulled her shirt off over her head, and even all the way over here, I could see the way her tits bounced in the night air. Fuck, she was pretty. Her darkly tanned skin fucking glowed in the firelight. Draining my bottle, I snatched up the one Blondie had started. Considering I hadn't eaten all fucking day, the beer was going straight to my head. Which probably wasn't such a hot idea, but I didn't give a fuck. When the man in front of Missy wrapped his hands around her lush mounds and started sucking on her nipples, a growl rolled out of me. Those were mine, dammit. Not fucking his.

When the men moved Missy onto all fours and filled her mouth and pussy with their cocks, I couldn't stand it any longer. Pulling Blondie off my cock, I turned her around so she was on all fours like Missy, and after ripping her thong away, I thrust in deep and pounded her hard, wishing on every fucking stroke that it was my Missy I was plowing into, not some whore whose name I couldn't even remember.

Missy

In the six months I'd been at the Charon MC clubhouse, I'd settled into the life with ease. Club life was similar to the commune, in that it was separate from the real world. It was safe here for me to relax and enjoy myself. It also helped that for the most part, we club whores all got along well, except for a couple who thought they were God's gift to men. The turnover of the ones like that was pretty high though, so it wasn't too hard to put up with them. It seemed that the men figured out what those women were playing at pretty quickly, and they used them hard and roughly once they did. Not many of them lasted long after that crap started.

Despite Scout's warning that I was going to be used hard and often, it hadn't happened. Well, at least after the first few weeks it hadn't. Those weeks had been eye opening, that's for sure. The Charon MC men were pretty much all big and muscular, and they had near insatiable appetites for sex. But the main difference between here and back at the compound was that these men gave back, some more than others. Even though we were just the whores, the men never hurt us. Well, some of the girls liked a bit of pain with their fucking, but aside from that, the men never hurt us. Since being here, I'd never been hit, punched or slapped. Nor had I ever been spoken to in a way that left me wanting to scrub the skin from my bones. Sure, once the brothers started getting drunk they got more crude and cussed more, but they never degraded me to the point I wanted to fade from existence, like I had as a teenager.

Except for one thing, I loved life here at the Charon MC clubhouse. That one thing was Tiny. Damn, but he was a beautiful man. Messy dark hair, scruffy beard and soulful hazel eyes I could stare into all damn day. And despite his road-name, he wasn't small in the least. Nope, he was huge, like a bear. He wasn't only tall at six feet five, but broad in the shoulders, too. When he came for me, I adored how he'd hold me against him. It felt like he'd keep me safe from everything when he wrapped me up in his big arms. His size easily dwarfed me, but I never felt intimidated. Nope, I felt safe. Protected.

A sigh escaped me as I made my way back to the bar for more drinks to take back out there. He didn't search me out much anymore. Fawn, another of the club whores who I lived with, told me it was because he wanted me for more than some quick relief. But if that were the case, wouldn't he be all over me whenever he could? Fawn said that was why I didn't get chosen by the others very often, because they didn't want to piss Tiny off. Well, they pissed me off. Since coming to the Charons, I'd discovered I rather liked sex. For all the training I'd received in the commune, I'd never been allowed to enjoy the act myself. It had always been all about what the man wanted. Here, with these men, it was mutual. Sure, I was expected to follow orders and make sure the men came, but I was allowed to enjoy it too. Enjoy being the center of someone's attention, for at least a little while. So when I got left in the corner while all the other girls were busy getting some attention, I couldn't help but feel like there was something wrong with me. Especially when I was forced to stand by and watch Tiny be with the others.

That's why I liked these weekends. Whenever the Satan's Cowboys came to town I knew I was in for a busy time. So when the clock had first hit ten about an hour ago, and I'd followed the others out to the bonfire, I hadn't been surprised to be snatched up by a couple of the Cowboys and taken care of within minutes. My pussy tingled and I smiled at the memory of having the two of them all over me. They'd helped me feel like a woman again.

Once I had my hands full of opened bottles—I'd now worked out how to take four without spilling anything—I went back toward the yard. Once there, I started handing out the drinks. Scout took one and gave my ass a tap in thanks as I moved on. The second bottle went to a younger guy, a prospect who was quick to pull me in close before he tugged my top down and latched onto my nipple for a minute after he'd slipped a bottle from my grip. Next thing I knew, the other bottles were being lifted from my grip. Then, two large hands slid up my thighs and gripped handfuls of my ass, before they moved to hold my hips.

"Damn, you are a pretty little thing aren't ya, sugar?"

I knew the voice. It was Keg, one of the brothers who spent a lot of time in the whore room. He drew me back from the prospect, who didn't look happy but didn't say anything as he drank his beer and watched. It hadn't taken me long to realize that prospects didn't rank too high in this place. If a patched in brother wanted me, the prospect had no chance of having me.

I was pulled back against a hard body and large, rough hands came around to my front. He rolled my shirt up so that both of my breasts were now on display. I moaned at the feel of the night air brushing over my sensitive skin. Then he squeezed and tugged on my nipples until the arousal spiraling through my system had me grinding my ass against him. He kept his teasing up, tugging and pinching my flesh, until I was on the edge of an orgasm.

"You gonna fuck me, or what?"

"Oh, not me. I'm just testing a theory here, and our boy is about to prove me right. You can come thank me later, sugar."

Confusion brought me back from the edge a fraction, but before I could ask what the hell he meant, he turned me away from the prospect and toward the fire.

Toward Tiny.

"Oh, fuck."

I tried to back away, but Keg released my breasts and wrapped his palms around my hips, holding me still as he softly kissed my throat below my ear. Tiny's lips kicked up into a sneer as he strode toward us, focusing on where Keg was touching me with his mouth.

"Please, Keg, just let me go already."

I had to get away. I'd seen Tiny fucking another of the whores earlier, and as usual, it had cut me down to my soul. I couldn't take a run-in with him now. Keg had gotten me so worked up, but now that arousal was turning and twisting into something else. Something, that, if I gave in and let it loose, would get me kicked out of the clubhouse. I'd been told not to let my heart get involved here. I knew I couldn't lay any real claim to the man currently coming at me like an out-of-control freight train.

"Shh, Missy, you'll be fine. He wouldn't ever hurt you, babe. Now, he might take a swing at me for this, but we gotta get him past whatever shit he's hung up on that's stopping him from doing the right thing with you."

I shook my head, but didn't have time to ask anything else before a furious Tiny stood before me. His gaze dropped down and caught on my breasts for a minute, like he couldn't help himself.

"Hey, Tiny, you're looking a little vicious there, brother. I'm sure Missy, here, can help you with that. Ain't that right Missy?"

Keg's palms covered my breasts again and the vein

above Tiny's right eye started to pulse. His eyes were glazed with a drunken gleam and I really wasn't sure what he was going to do next. What I did know, was that Keg was playing with fucking fire and dangling me right over the top of the damn flames.

I jumped with a squeal when he threw his bottle in the nearby bin hard enough it shattered others as it landed. Once again I tried to back away, but Keg's hard body wouldn't budge. I was caught between two lions and I really felt like a little mouse right about now. Keg wasn't as tall as Tiny, but he was still a lot taller than my five feet three height.

"Please..."

I honestly didn't know what I wanted to happen, but this tension was killing me. My body was still strung tightly from not getting the release Keg had teased me with earlier. The fact I could now smell Tiny's scent wasn't helping, even if he didn't look like he wanted to help me out.

With a growl, Tiny reached for me. When his large palm wrapped around my arm, Keg released me with a chuckle.

"Glad to see you manning up, brother. Go take care of her."

Then Keg was gone and it was just Tiny and me. The big man who had unintentionally stolen my heart from me. It had been over a week since he'd searched me out and I'd missed his touch, his scent. All the men smelled of leather, but Tiny had an extra spice to his scent that could make me wet just from the smell.

I didn't know what the hell Keg had meant with his words, but I could see Tiny was on edge. Would he let me ease him back down? With a twitch of my hips, I slid up against his front. He'd taken off his shirt at some point, and his muscular chest and abs peaked out from the center of his cut. When his grip on my arm loosened, I ran my palms up under his cut so I could press my exposed breasts against his bare chest. A moan bubbled up from my throat when my nipples scraped against his hard torso. He stiffened beneath my touch, and a flash of panic flared inside me that he was going to shove me away and leave. Before he could, I ran a palm down to the large bulge behind his fly and gave him a squeeze.

"Want me to take care of this for you, babe?"

Something dark flashed in his eyes before, with a growl, he lifted me up and slung me over his shoulder. Men laughed around us as he strode for the door. His palm was wrapped around my upper thigh, his fingers oh-so-close to where I wanted him. With a deep breath, I pushed my arousal aside, and lifting my head, noticed he was heading for the stairs. He was taking me to his room? I chewed on my lower lip at what this could mean. Normally club whores didn't get the privacy of a room. Generally speaking, the bikers just fucked us where they found us. I couldn't help but hope that maybe Tiny did feel something more for me.

A few minutes later, I was dropped on a large bed. I kept my gaze locked on my man, waiting for something to happen. Like, maybe the alarm going off and me waking up, because this all felt like something I'd dream up.

In silence I watched him peel off his cut, hang it up, then strip out of his boots and jeans. I nearly swallowed my tongue. I'd never seen him completely naked before. He was a work of art, and not just because of all the ink. My fingers itched to touch and caress, but I didn't want to risk breaking whatever spell he was under.

When he took hold of my ankle and tugged me to the edge of the bed, a little squeak of surprise left me and he grinned.

"Kinda like you making that sound, Missy."

He pulled me up to stand and made fast work of stripping me bare.

"However, what I don't like is the smell of other men on what's mine. Come with me."

His words were slightly slurred, and I hoped like hell he wasn't so drunk that he'd forget about this in the morning. If he pulled a stunt like that, I wasn't sure I'd survive it. Not after having him call me his, like he just had.

Chapter 2

Missy

The shower had been short and hot. Clearly impatient, Tiny had guided me under the spray before it was warm, but his roaming hands made sure I didn't give a damn about the temperature of the water spraying down on us. And my own hands had been far from idle, as I'd made the most of the opportunity and ran my fingers over every inch of him I could reach.

Now I stood in his room, waiting for him to return. He'd run a towel over me, and was currently tossing it back into the bathroom. In seconds he was back on me, wrapping me up in his big arms. My heart melted as he surrounded my smaller body with his larger one. When he lifted me up, I wrapped my legs around his waist and my arms around his neck. We both groaned when my slick pussy came up against the tight muscles of his abs. He buried his face against my throat and inhaled.

"Hmm, that's better. Fuck, you smell so good, babe."

He lifted me higher so he could get his mouth on my breast. When the wet heat of his mouth engulfed the tip, I twisted my hips against him, trying to get more friction against my clit, as he had my arousal once again spiraling close to climax.

With a growl, he dropped me, making me squeak again as I landed on the bed with a light bounce. Entranced, I couldn't take my gaze from his face. He looked like a wild animal, ready to devour his prey. Lifting my hand, I curled a finger at him to come to me. And like the good boy he was, he did as I asked. With a knee on the bed between my thighs, he crawled over me, kissing and nipping his way up my body. When he got level with my face, he took my mouth, and I nearly cried. Tiny had never kissed me before. Not many of the men wanted to kiss us whores. It wasn't normally part of the deal of fucking. His lips were so soft, and they melded against mine like we'd been made for each other. After he lightly nipped my lower lip, he pushed himself up and rolled off me. Before I could get upset at him rejecting me, he hauled me over on top of him.

"Want you on top, babe. Wanna see these tits of yours bounce as you ride my cock."

With a grin on my face and a buzz running through my blood, I slid up his body until I could lean back and take his dick inside me. I didn't need foreplay with Tiny—one glance at the big man and I was wet and willing. After the shower and his kiss, I was definitely wet enough to take his big cock within me easily.

Once I was fully seated on his length, I straightened up, then arched my back as bliss flowed through me.

"Feels so good, Tiny. Only you fill me like this."

Instead of verbally responding, he gripped my hips and lifted me up before pushing me down again, setting the pace even though I was on top. I swiveled and tilted my hips in time with his movements, and through hooded lids watched as his gaze stayed latched onto my breasts. Feeling sexy as fuck, I lifted my palms to cup and play with the mounds. Moments later, he sat up and wrapped his mouth around first one, then the other. He sucked and bit at my nipples until I was mindlessly whimpering as I ground my pussy on his cock.

"Please, Tiny, I need to come so bad."

He lifted his head, and with a wicked grin, rolled us over so I was now under him. Pulling free from my body, he shifted until he was standing beside the bed, before he moved me so I was in front of him. Hooking my legs over his elbows, he spread me wider and thrust back in deep. My back arched up as I gripped fists full of the bedding on a silent scream. His dick was as big as the rest of him, and with me spread out like this, he went deeper. His thrusts sped up until he was pounding into me, my breasts bouncing with each thrust, and I could feel his hot gaze watching them move.

Sweat broke out over his body, making him glow in the dim light of the room. Knowing he was close had me closer than ever. I reached a hand down and rubbed my clit. Just as my body came alive and blew apart with my orgasm, I felt him jerk within me, heard him growl as he came deep inside me, filling me up with his seed.

If only I wasn't on the shot.

If only I wasn't nothing but a club whore he couldn't stand the thought of taking for his old lady.

With a groan, he dropped his weight on me, and tears pricked my eyes before they flowed down my cheeks. The intensity of my climax together with the realization that Tiny would never really claim me, had me falling completely apart as I shuddered beneath him.

He jerked and rolled off me, and the bed. "Oh, shit. Did I hurt you, Missy? Fuck. I was too rough and you're so small. *Shit.*"

I shook my head. "Not hurt, just overwhelmed."

I held my arms out toward him, hoping he'd embrace me and cuddle for a few minutes before he booted me out the door.

"Thank fuck. Don't ever wanna hurt you, Missy."

He crawled back onto the bed, and with an arm around my middle, dragged me with him until both our heads were on the pillow. He reached down and flipped the blankets over us before he killed the bedside light.

"Get some rest, sugar. Pretty sure I'm gonna be waking you back up soon. Can't seem to fucking get enough of you."

I silently blinked over at him in shock. He wanted to actually *sleep* with me? No man had ever wanted me for more than a blow job or fuck. I didn't want to screw this up so I wasn't sure what to do.

He chuckled softly. "Don't look so fucking scared, babe. I ain't gonna hurt ya. Just don't want you to go yet.

I like how you fit in my arms."

Did I dare admit how I was feeling?

"I've never felt like this, like I do when you hold me. It's like I'm truly safe when you surround me."

He gave me a dopey looking grin, and I guessed between the alcohol and the orgasm he just had, he was about to pass out on me.

"This is all new to me too, babe. But I like holding you too, and ain't nothing gonna hurt you while I'm around. Don't you worry about that. Now, come over here and let me hold you."

Nervously, I slipped over until I was pressed in tight to his side, with half of my body over his front. He took my palm and placed it over his heart, before covering it with his own, then he pressed the most reverent kiss I'd ever had to the top of my head before he relaxed back and went to sleep.

Despite being tired myself, sleep didn't come easily. I lay there watching him for ages, memorizing every breath he took and hoping like hell this wasn't some kind of dream, until finally sleep claimed me.

The growl that awoke me hours later was not a happy sound. Squinting against the bright light coming in through the window, I rolled over and rubbed my face.

"What the fuck?"

Tiny's rough voice had every ounce of sleep vanishing from my system in an instant. Slowly I turned to face him and found him standing by the bed pulling his jeans up while glaring at me. My eyes stung but I refused to let any tears fall. He didn't deserve to see that he'd hurt me. *So much for his promise.*

"Guess you were so drunk last night you don't remember dragging me up here, huh?"

With false bravado, I spoke the words like my heart wasn't currently shattering within my chest. Scout had warned me to not fall for any of the brothers. But I had. And now, I was paying the price. I slipped from beneath the blankets and quickly dressed. I needed to get out of here and leave the clubhouse before any of the old ladies with kids came around for any reason. Who was I kidding? I needed to get the fuck outta here before I couldn't hold myself together any longer.

The fact that Tiny didn't utter another word as I dressed and left his room made it both worse and better at the same time. There wasn't much he could have said that would have improved the situation, but the fact he didn't care I was leaving? That shit stung.

As I made the short walk back to the house I shared with a few of the other girls, my mind played back every interaction I'd ever had with Tiny. Every touch and fuck, every word we'd shared. Every time I'd seen him fucking another of the whores. By the time I unlocked the front door and walked in, my chest felt like it was on fire. Pain radiated through my body with every step. When I turned to close the door on my bedroom, I half expected to see a trail of my blood down the hallway, but nope, my pain was all internal.

With a quiet snick, the door shut and I leaned against

it, resting my forehead on the smooth surface. What was I going to do? Could I face Tiny again after last night and this morning? I had doubts my heart could take watching him with the others now that I'd fully lost my stupid fucking heart to him.

Tiny

Fortunately for me, within hours of Missy leaving my bed, I'd had to go on another run. Being one of the club's enforcers kept me busy, that's for sure. This one had been a big one, taking us six days. So, it was nearly a week after that cluster fuck of a night and morning with Missy that I was sitting in Styxx, the bar owned by the Charons, drinking beer I had to fucking pay for because I was too chicken-shit to go back to the clubhouse after ten and deal with the mess I'd made with Missy, when Keg came after me.

"You stupid, fucking asshole. What the hell did you do to her?"

I raised a single eyebrow at him as I took another drink.

"No fucking clue what you're talking about."

That had him on the verge of vibrating with rage. He stormed right up to me, until he was only inches away from my face. Taking a fist full of my shirt, he pulled back his other hand to take a swing. That had me moving. Standing to my full height had him dropping his grip and shaking his head at me. Keg was a big bastard, and another of the club's enforcers, but I was bigger and stronger than he was. He'd also been on the run with me, so I had no fucking clue what had his panties in a twist so soon after we pulled in.

"You know what? You ain't worth the trouble I'd cop for beating your skull in. But it's what you fucking deserve, asshole."

Anger, and a good dose of embarrassment, had my blood heating and left me itching for a fight.

"What the fuck is your issue? We've been back what? An hour tops and you've already found some fucking drama to come bust my balls over? What the fuck?"

"Well someone has to! I guess from the fact you're fucking clueless as to why I've come for your ass, you don't realize that Missy fucking left while we were gone?"

That had my full attention, and drained all the anger out of me instantly. I dropped down into my seat and frowned over at Keg as he stayed standing.

"What do you mean she's gone?"

Keg started pacing, throwing his hands up in the air as he muttered to himself for a while.

"Keg! Quit fucking around, where's Missy?"

He spun on me with a furious expression. "No one fucking knows! Fawn came and found me when I got in tonight. She was in one hell of a state because Scout, you and me were all on that run all week, so she had no fucking clue who to tell that Missy packed up her stuff and left by the time Fawn got up Monday morning. So, I repeat my initial question—what the fuck did you do to that woman before we left?"

A mix of pain and panic loosened my tongue. "You're one to fucking talk. It was you who pushed me last Sunday night. I would never have taken her up to my room, otherwise."

He just shook his head at me. "Taking her to your room was about the only fucking thing you did right, by the looks of it. Tell me, why isn't she still there? Why you here paying for your booze when it flows free at the clubhouse?"

I didn't like Keg hitting so close to the truth. "Fawn talks too much."

"That girl doesn't talk enough. The second she realized Missy had left, she should have gone to one of the others. And today she was waiting for you to show your face. Guess after she saw the rest of us come in without you she gave up and got desperate to tell someone who might give a fuck."

Which would be Keg. Now that Taz had settled down, Keg was the one who spent the most time in the whore room. He was the one they trusted the most. I scrubbed my face in my palms. I had a curious pain in my chest at the thought of never seeing Missy again.

"Fawn say why she didn't go to Taz, or one of the other brothers?"

Just because Taz had an old lady now, didn't mean he didn't give a fuck about the fact one of the girls had gone missing.

"Yeah, said that she knows how the whores come and go from the clubhouse, and that the club officers likely wouldn't give a shit one had moved on. But Fawn was her friend, knew her well enough to know she had nowhere to go if she left. And like everyone else, she saw you carry her off Sunday night."

There were two types of club whores, ones like Fawn who stuck around no matter what, and ones who floated in and out. We all knew from day one that Missy wouldn't be one of the ones who disappeared on the regular.

"Have you told Scout?"

He shook his head. "She's your damn woman, not mine. You gonna step the fuck up here? Or are you still caught up in your head? Because if you are, maybe you should just forget about her and let her go. She's strong, she'll find somewhere new to settle down and have a life."

Keg turned and left, and I sat back and finished my beer while my mind spun with thoughts. Did she really have no one to go to out in the world, like me? If that was the case, where the fuck did she go? I felt like a fucking bastard for never having asked her anything. I thought about the woman pretty much twenty-four/seven, yet I'd never bothered to even ask her what her real name was.

Shame filled me. I didn't deserve her with the way I'd acted.

The more I drank, the clearer that thought became.

But it wasn't the only one. Missy was a little thing, only a little over five feet tall, and so delicate. Was she really strong enough to survive out in the world on her own? I wasn't so sure. Then there was the real question of the evening—was *I* fucking strong enough to man up and go get her back? If I did, I knew things would have to change. I couldn't go round her up and deposit her back in the whore room with the others. Just because I didn't admit it to Keg, it didn't change the fact that I'd been an asshole when I'd woken up hung over to discover she was sleeping beside me like some kind of fallen angel. That's what made her run. I couldn't remember much about what I'd said in my drunken state Sunday night, but I could take a guess that I'd been a little too honest with her. Then Monday morning I'd woken up cursing her. I hadn't bothered to try to explain what was going on in my head. Nope, I'd stayed silent as she'd rushed to dress while she tried to hide her emotions. Only a fucking moron would have missed the tears in her eyes. But did I do anything about it? Nope. I just stood there in silence and watched her. No wonder she ran. Hell, if I could run from myself, I would have too that morning.

Fuck.

Dropping some bills on the table, I stood and left Styxx. I needed to find Scout, see who interviewed her when she came on board. They might know where she'd headed off to.

Chapter 3

Tiny

"What the fuck do you mean she left six fucking days ago?"

Scout's fury had me taking a step back. While I hadn't expected the president to be happy about Missy vanishing, I hadn't expected him to react like this.

"I only just found out myself. I, ah, Monday morning didn't end well for us. I didn't check in with her before we left for the run, and when we got back I went straight to Styxx."

Scout readjusted his bandana while grumbling under his breath several threats I hoped he didn't intend to try out on me. Before I could ask him why Missy was so important to him, he pulled his phone out and made a call.

"Hey, Keys, I need you to find Missy for me. She packed up and vanished Monday morning—" With a wince Scout pulled the phone away from his ear. "I'm aware that was six fucking days ago. Quit bitching about it and fucking do it already. Also, check if there's been any action this past week near that fucking commune in Soule that I asked you to look into." He paused again. "Yeah, that's right. Missy is Mercedes Soto and that commune is her fucked-up stepfamily. Keep me updated with whatever you find. I told that girl I'd keep her safe, and I don't fucking break my promises."

He was glaring at me when he said that last part, but my mind was too busy spinning with what he'd just said to be worried about the fact my president was pissed off at me. As soon as he hung up the phone, I started asking questions.

"Missy came from a fucking commune and you never told us?"

He raised a single brow at me and I got the feeling I'd stepped way over a line I shouldn't have just now.

"Don't forget who you're fucking talking to, boy. Missy freely came to me wanting to be one of the whores here at the clubhouse. I offered her other work, but she wasn't comfortable enough in the outside world to take it. I'm not sure what the fuck they did to her in that commune she grew up in, but obviously it included sexual training. Because from the moment she came through our doors, it was the whore room she had her eye on and she's not once batted an eye at filling her obligations. Pretty sure it's no fucking commune she came from, but a cult, which is why I've had Keys looking into it."

"Why'd she run in the first place?"

That earned me another glare from my president.

"We find her? You can't let on that you know any of this shit, you get me? She didn't want anyone knowing about her past."

I nodded. "I won't say a word."

"And if I tell you why she ran in the first place, you need to cop to whatever the fuck you did that sent her running."

With a wince, I gave him another nod. "Okay."

"She came home one day to find her mother on the verge of death. She used her last breaths to tell her daughter to run like hell and never look back. She did. Your turn."

I rubbed a hand over the back of my neck. What could I say?

"I was pretty fucking polluted Sunday, and I ended up taking Missy up to my room for the night. When I woke up cursing, hung over as shit, she panicked and fled. I didn't try to stop her." I frowned. "I didn't think it would send her running. I mean, sure, I figured she'd be pissed with me for a while, but I didn't think it would send her out the fucking door."

Scout was shaking his head. "You're a fucking moron. I tell every single one of those girls not to lose their fucking hearts to any of the men here, but some of them can't seem to help it. And Missy fell for your dumb ass months ago. Don't suppose you can remember what happened Sunday night? What you said to her?"

Again, I shook my head. "I remember getting pissed off at the Cowboys fucking her, then when Keg started in on her, I saw red. Took her up to my room and fucked her, but I've got no idea what I might have said to her."

Scout crossed his arms over his chest and leaned back in his seat. "You've got some decisions to make, Tiny. I intend on finding her no matter what you decide. But, what I do when I find her is up to you. Do you want her for your old lady? Because if not, I'm just going to make sure she's okay, then leave her be."

That ache I'd had in my chest since Monday flared up again as though someone had just shoved a hot poker in there.

"I never wanted an old lady, Scout. Saw enough of how it is to have a woman full time when I was growing up in foster care. All that fucking drama. No way do I want to have to live like that."

Scout shifted in his seat, looking uncomfortable as he readjusted his bandana. Again.

"I cannot believe I'm the one who has to tell you this shit." He paused to clear his throat. "Right. Well, listen up because I'm only telling you this shit once. Not every relationship is the same. And not all turn toxic. Just look around you, for fuck's sake. Bulldog and Rose have been going strong for over two decades. I've known them since they were dating and I've never once seen those two get into each other. Keys and Donna? They buried their daughter last year, but together they're dealing with the grief and moving forward. One thing I can guarantee you? You'll regret not taking this chance when you get older. Trust me on that one. So, Tiny, you've got until

Keys gets here with whatever information he's found, to figure out what you're gonna do. But if you don't intend on claiming her as your own, you ain't coming with us. Understand?"

"Yeah, I hear you. I'm gonna go grab a shower and get cleaned up."

"Sounds good. If you're coming with us, we'll be heading out as soon as I know what direction to ride."

I made my way up to my room on autopilot. Was it worth the risk? I ran through all the current couples in the club, and got stuck thinking about Taz and Flick. Taz had been the biggest man-whore in the club before Flick came and knocked him on his ass. Now they were expecting a baby and Taz seemed happy enough. Actually, I couldn't recall ever seeing him without a grin lately. Eagle and Mac were both dads now too, and they both seemed pretty content with their new role in life. An image of Missy flashed across my mind. She was so fucking pretty. Did she want kids? A family? Or was she happy being a club whore.

A growl tore up my throat. Of course she wasn't fucking happy being a whore. Very few women were, and if she was, she wouldn't have left. I slammed into my room and stripped as I entered the bathroom. Flipping on the taps, all I could see was her in here. Fuck, I'd dragged her in here to wash the smell of the other men off her before I fucked her. I really needed to quit getting so polluted that I couldn't fucking remember shit the next day. What the hell had I said to her?

Once I was done, I headed back out to get dressed and caught sight of the messed up bed. I'd slept like shit this past week on the road. Funny, when I'd had Missy sleeping wrapped around me, I'd slept like a dead man. As I pulled my cut on over my shoulders, I realized I was being a fucking idiot. My brain might be still arguing the truth, but my stupid, fucking heart had jumped ship long ago.

Mercedes Soto was mine. All mine. And I needed to man the fuck up and be who she needed me to be. The instant I made the decision, accepted the truth, the weight on my chest that had been crushing me for so long, lightened. I knew I had a shit-ton of work ahead of me. We might not even be able to find the woman, and if we did, there was a good chance she wouldn't want to see me. Especially since I still couldn't fucking remember exactly what I'd done or said that sent her running.

With purpose, I trotted back down the stairs and headed for Scout's office. With a tap on the door frame, I strolled in to find Keys there, staring at his laptop with a serious expression.

"I'm done screwing around. Missy is mine and I'm gonna do whatever I have to do to get her back here where she fucking belongs."

Keys shook his head at me. "About fucking time. Now, get over here. I spoke with Fawn and once I had a rough idea of what time she left worked out, it didn't take me long to piece together her movements. She caught a bus to Houston. Then with Fawn's help, and hacking into a few surveillance-video feeds, I've tracked her to a strip club on the outskirts of Houston, called Sexy Legs."

My gut dropped at the thought of how many men were looking at what was mine, that I'd been the bastard that had pushed her to it. "Why there? She couldn't have just stumbled upon the place and gotten a job."

"Another of the whores used to work there. Fawn's heard her talking about it, so it's easy to assume that Missy had overheard the same information."

The fact that no one was heading to their bikes had me frowning. "Why aren't we moving out then?"

"Because that's not the only issue in this fucked-up situation, brother. Her stepfather is on the move. He was spotted with a small group heading toward Bridgewater yesterday, but I haven't been able to get a bead on him since then."

"In the six months she's been here, has he ever shown any sign that he's been looking for her?"

Keys glanced at Scout, who nodded, before he turned back to me. "They've put out some feelers for her. Her stepfather is claiming she's his runaway daughter that he wants to bring back home. He spins a good story, but then most of these guys do. It's how they draw so many people in to their fucked-up communes in the first place."

"Has he been seen here in town?"

"No fucking way. If he'd dared step one foot in our town we would have dealt with the fucker in a heartbeat."

The sense of urgency I felt increased the more I thought about what could happen.

"So, why are we still sitting here and not already on our way to Houston?"

"I was just setting up things for after, while we waited for you to make the right decision and get your ass back down here."

I started for the door. "Well, I'm here, now let's go. Who's coming with us?"

Not that I cared. I'd go alone if I had to. And if Missy's stepfather had gotten hold of her, I wasn't sure what I was going to do to the bastard, but it wouldn't be pretty.

Missy

At the end of each day for the past four days, after I'd finished work and finally got to slip into the crappy, lumpy bed in the small room above Sexy Legs to try to sleep, I would question my decision of leaving Bridgewater and the Charon MC. Maybe I should've just gone straight to Scout, rather than leaving, and asked about working somewhere else. He'd offered me other jobs when I'd first come to the club. Surely one of those options would have still been available.

But instead, I'd run like a coward, letting a man run me off with a few careless words. Tiny had been hung over as hell. Maybe he hadn't even meant what he'd said to me. That, or he hadn't meant what he'd said the night before. What he'd said while he was drunk. Although, in my experience, drunk people were more likely to tell you the truth than sober ones.

At least I wasn't on the streets. I'd overheard a couple of the other girls at the clubhouse talking about working shifts at Sexy Legs, so when I saw the neon sign from the bus, I headed in that direction. Considering I was used to not only taking off my clothes, but fucking for food and a roof over my head, stripping didn't seem like such a bad gig. And at the mention of my previous employment, the owner hadn't hesitated to hire me.

But it wasn't time for me to head upstairs yet tonight. I still had work to do. And as I did another twirl around the pole, I realized I didn't get the buzz doing anything in this place like I'd gotten when I strutted around the Charon MC clubhouse. And when I slid to the floor to crawl around the front of the stage so the men, and women, there, could tuck money into my thong, their touches made my skin crawl. Maybe it was the nastiness and cruelty mixed with the lust in so many of their gazes. The Charons had never been like that. If they wanted me, they took me, but they were never nasty about it. No, the men here reminded me more of those back in the commune. Of the teachers who trained me, and the boys in the class who would watch as we girls were put through sexual test after test. A shudder ran through me and I performed a body roll to hide it from those watching me.

When the last notes of the song I'd been dancing to finished, I went to move off stage, but as I did a final twirl I saw him. No, it wasn't just him, but them. He'd brought several of his friends with him. My throat dried up and my feet wouldn't move. I hadn't seen or heard anything from him in so long. How had he found me?

When the next girl came out cussing at me to get my ass off stage, I spun and bolted down the stairs, pulling the bills free from my thong as I strode down the hallway to the little room we all used to change. I was due to perform again in an hour, but I didn't want to risk it with my stepfamily out there. Had they seen me yet? Maybe I could sneak out the back and run. But to where? Would Scout take me back after I left without telling anyone? Considering I hadn't heard from any of them all week, I had to wonder if they'd even noticed I'd gone. Maybe I could slip back in and act like I'd never left.

Decision made, I grabbed my stuff and headed up to my room. Unsure how cold it was outside, I quickly changed into a pair of jeans, sneakers and threw on a t-shirt and jacket before shoving everything else back in my bag. I scribbled a quick note to my boss and left half of the money I'd collected tonight with it. That was a lot more than his normal cut, so hopefully he wouldn't be too mad. There were plenty of other girls here to take the stage in my place, so I was fairly certain he wouldn't even notice my absence until after closing.

With my bag over my shoulder, I slipped down the stairs and out the rear door. Keeping to the shadows, I made my way to the side of the building. Sexy Legs was on the outskirts of town, and there was a truck stop not far down the road. Hopefully I could hitch a ride without too much trouble and be far from here before my stepfather realized I'd slipped past him.

"Hello, Mercedes. Where do you think you're going?"

The breath caught in my lungs as I suddenly found myself surrounded by men from the commune. Front and center, naturally, was my stepfather.

"What do you want?"

"I wanted to bring you home so you could take the place you were trained to take, but I'm not sure you deserve that now. Not with how you killed your mother, then ran away to use your training to be a stripper."

Fury spiked my blood and banished my fear. I lunged for him, wanting to scratch his eyes out for his lies, but strong hands held me back.

"*You* killed her, not me. You and your friends beat and used her until she was too broken to be used anymore, then you left her there for me to find!"

I pulled and twisted, trying to get free of the men who held me, but they were stronger and so much bigger than me. How could they stand so stoic against his lies? Hell, these were probably the ones who'd used my mother until she was a whisper away from death, then left her to die.

"Such a wild imagination you have, Mercedes. Take her out behind that shed, boys. We don't need strangers interfering in our family business now, do we?"

As they moved, I did everything I could to dig my heels into the gravel parking lot to slow them down. I turned my head toward the road and opened my mouth to scream. But before any sound came out, a hand clamped over my mouth.

"Don't you think you've pissed him off enough already, girl?"

Tears pricked my eyes, but I refused to allow them to fall. I was going to be raped and beaten, most likely until I stopped breathing, behind that shed. And they wanted me to go quietly? Like hell. I might have only been out of that commune for six months, but it had been long enough for me to learn that the way they treated women, and how they forced them to behave was wrong. We weren't meant to be slaves to the men around us our whole lives. Hell, even as a club whore for the Charon MC I had more freedom than what I'd had in that commune.

My gaze bounced around the parking lot. I had to find a way to escape, to get someone's attention before they got me out of sight. Suddenly I could hear the faint sound of several Harleys. They were getting louder as they got closer and the sound made my heart sing, I seriously doubted the bikes were the Charons, but I didn't care. If they were cut from the same cloth, they'd never leave a woman in trouble.

"Hurry up!"

The two men holding my arms tightened their grips to

a painful level and two more men came and grabbed my legs. Screaming, I thrashed against their hold but it got me nowhere, and now I had nothing touching the ground I had no way of slowing them down as they carried me out of the dimly lit lot and behind an old shed at the rear of the yard. The bikes were loud now, as if they were maybe pulling into the lot. I tried to twist around to see them but couldn't catch more than a glimpse of big black and silver machines before I was taken out of sight.

"Pin her up against the wall. Gonna have to make this a quick lesson, then we'll take her home to finish off."

True to my stepfather's instructions, my feet were dropped and the two holding my arms, thrust me up against the rough metal. The breath rushed from my lungs, but I didn't take my gaze from my stepfather. Fury and desperation had banished all my fear, numbing my body against what I knew was coming.

"I'm not yours, not anymore. You have no right to touch me and when the Charon MC finds out what you've done, you'll all be dead. You have heard of the club haven't you?"

With a growl, he stepped forward and viciously backhanded me across my face, hard enough to have me seeing stars.

"You whored yourself out to an entire motorcycle club? That's how you've stayed hidden so long." He scoffed, and taking a fist full of my shirt, gave it a hard yank and ripped the front out of it, leaving my bra exposed. "They'll probably thank me for taking you off their hands. Considering you're not at their clubhouse anymore, I'm guessing they got sick of you and tossed you aside." He pulled a knife from his belt and sliced the center of my bra open. "Now for some fun, my little whore."

When he slipped the blade under the top of my jeans, slicing through the denim, I let out the loudest scream I could. The bikes had been shut off for a few minutes now, and I prayed that at least one of them would hear me and come investigate.

Whoever they were, they were my only hope.

Chapter 4

Tiny

We rolled into the strip club's parking lot just as a group of men were walking toward the rear of the lot. They looked like they were struggling with something, but in the dark I couldn't see what it was. At least, not until our headlights flashed over the group. They had Missy. *Fuck.* Were we too late?

Scout was in the lead and he held up his fist, like he knew I wanted to ride over there and plow into the bastards with my bike. Then he pointed to the side where there was plenty of space for us to all park our rides together. The second I had my bike parked, the engine was off and I had my helmet on my seat as I strode toward my girl.

"Tiny, wait!"

I turned to face Scout, pointing the direction they'd gone. "They've got her. Right this very second they're hurting my woman. Why the fuck should I wait?"

"Ten fucking seconds, Tiny. Do not kill them. We got plans for them and we need them to be breathing.

Understand?"

"No guarantees, prez. I'll try, but to keep her safe, I'll do anything. And I'm not feeling real rational right now."

"Fine, go get your girl. No fucking guns though. We don't have any contacts with the cops this far out of Bridgewater and I'd prefer avoid that headache if we can."

I gave him a chin lift just as a high pitched scream ripped through the air. *Oh, hell no.* I spun on my heel and sprinted across the gravel toward the sound. I could hear my brothers' feet pounding the ground behind me and knew they'd have my back, even if I decided to slaughter every one of these fuckers who'd dared to touch what was mine.

Despite the fact I knew what they'd be doing, the sight that greeted me when I got behind that fucking shed had my stomach churning and my vision going red for a few moments.

"Get the fuck away from my woman."

A few of the men standing around began to back away, and I saw from the corner of my eye that a couple of my brothers headed after them. The ones holding Missy stood proud, like they had every right to be doing what they were. The one standing in front of her glanced over his shoulder to me but didn't turn his body. Fucker pulled his arm back and landed a blow against her stomach that left her wheezing for breath as he laughed.

"She ain't yours. She ain't nothing but a useless whore we're about to put to good use."

The man was a fucking idiot, and might as well have waved a red flag in my face. Keys rested his palm on my shoulder as he spoke near my ear.

"That's her stepfather. Leave. Him. Alive. Trust me, what we have coming his way is gonna be so much worse than you killing him now."

I didn't bother answering him, just shrugged off his hand and strode forward. When I was only a step away, the fucker moved to the side to reveal the knife he now had pressed against her throat. Fear had her eyes wide open and she was clearly trying to push herself away from the blade that was already drawing blood as it cut into her skin, but the shed was stopping her from going anywhere.

Her shirt had been torn away beneath her jacket and the top of jeans had been sliced open far enough to reveal most of her bare mound. Had I been too late? Had they already raped her? Fury, mixed with agony and rage, blew up inside me and I moved before I realized what I was doing. In seconds, I had one hand wrapped around his wrist and the other in his hair, before I yanked him back from Missy as I crushed his wrist between my thumb and fingers. With a screech, he dropped the blade and started whimpering. Fuck that.

Releasing his most-likely broken wrist, I pulled back and landed a blow to his ribs that would have at least cracked a few of the fuckers.

"How's it feel on the other side of things, asshole?"

When he just whimpered and tears tracked down his

face I snarled in disgust.

"You're not worth the effort it would take to kill you. No idea what my brother has planned for you, but I bet it's gonna be fun to watch."

With that, I brought his face down as I brought my knee up, and with a crunch that shattered his nose, he fell lifeless to the ground. Leaving him where he landed, I turned back to the trio still against the shed.

"I'm not feeling real charitable at the moment boys, I'd suggest you let my woman go and fuck off."

As though they were waiting for instruction, they dropped their hands from Missy and dashed away. I knew Scout and Keys would handle them, or maybe Arrow and Keg. I really didn't give a fuck as I rushed forward to catch Missy as she tumbled toward the ground now that no one was holding her up. She was still struggling to breathe from being manhandled with such force, and her face was red and swollen on one side.

"Ah, fuck, babe. I am so fucking sorry. Never again. I promise. This'll never fucking happen again."

She seemed even smaller than normal when I lifted her against me. With a groan, she curled one arm around her stomach while the other reached for my neck. Unable to reach high enough, she took a fistful of my cut and buried her face against my chest. Her whole body was shuddering, and I hoped like fuck she was crying and not convulsing for some reason.

A couple years back, the club had kitted out a cage as a sort of makeshift ambulance. It had come in handy a number of times already and when the vehicle pulled into the lot, I strode over toward it, more than ready to let Donna, Keys' old lady who was a trained nurse, do her thing with my girl. The back doors opened and Bulldog jumped out and winced when he caught sight of me.

"Hop in, Tiny. We've got another cage coming for the trash and I'll ride your bike home."

More than happy to have the club's VP ride my bike, after I got Missy settled on the gurney, I pulled my keys out and tossed them over.

"Thanks, brother."

With a nod, he closed the doors on us, and whoever was driving revved the engine as I sat down next to Missy and stroked her hair as Donna started to do her thing.

"It'll be okay, baby. We'll get you home, back where you belong."

She was still shaking and had a wild look in her eyes when I leaned in to kiss her forehead. When I pulled back, I saw Donna inject her with something that had her body relaxing and her eyes closing within seconds.

"Don't worry, it's just a light sedative. You doing okay, Tiny?"

I scrubbed a palm over the back of my neck. "Not really, Donna. Gonna be a good, long while before I'll be able to close my eyes and not see her like that—eyes wide in fear and her clothes all torn. Can you tell if they raped her?"

I glanced up to Donna as she clicked her tongue

before she answered.

"Her jeans were around her thighs, holding her legs together, so I doubt it, but I don't want to go doing anything invasive to her at this stage. She's gone through enough, and it won't help her heal for me to do it now." She paused as she took a pair of scissors and sliced down each side of Missy's jeans to remove them completely. She then made a quick inspection of her from foot to hip before pulling a blanket over her. "There's no clear sign of any injury to her lower half, aside from some bruising on her ankles, so I think it's best if we wait till she wakes up and ask her. If she was raped, then we'll deal with it."

My mind was a swirling mess of guilt, mixed in with rage. If only I hadn't been such an ass, she wouldn't have been at that club in the first place. Wouldn't have gotten hurt. I stroked her hair back from her face and lightly traced the swelling on her cheek. How could I have been so fucking cruel? I lowered my head to rest my forehead against hers as we drove the rest of the way back to the clubhouse.

Missy

With a groan, I slowly surfaced to consciousness. Damn, but I hurt all over. What the hell had happened last night? Blinking my eyes open, I saw I wasn't in my bed above Sexy Legs, but in a room at the clubhouse. *Oh, no.* I slowly turned my face and found Tiny standing beside the bed, shirtless with his arms folded over his broad chest and a thunderous look on his face. With a squeak, I jerked and tried to move away. I didn't remember how I ended up back in his bed, but I did not want a repeat of our last morning after. No way.

"Whoa, hey, Missy, stop. You'll hurt yourself."

Before I could get out of the bed, he was next to me, lying on the mattress with his arm keeping me flat on my back. I stilled, trying to process what was happening. Then, in a rush, my brain came online and memories of last night filtered through. Of seeing my stepfather at the club, of trying to run, then of being caught. With a gasp, I threw my arms around Tiny and pressed myself tight up against his big body, clinging to him as I fell apart. The tears came from nowhere but I couldn't stop them. He shifted, lifting me into his lap as he moved from lying down to sitting. He was so much bigger than me, I felt like a kitten in his lap as he kissed my head and stroked down my back with his large palm.

When the storm finally passed, I stayed pressed against him, stroking my fingers over his bare chest as I listened to his heart beat strong beneath my ear.

"I'm sorry."

At my hiccupped words, his body stiffened for a moment, before he hooked a finger under my jaw and tilted my face up so our gazes met. His pain and sorrow-filled gaze left me wincing.

"You've got nothing to be sorry for, sweetheart. I was the one who was a bastard and ran you off. I can't tell you how sorry I am. But why didn't you ever tell me about your past?"

I squeezed my eyes shut, unsure if this was real or if I was dreaming.

"I didn't want to think about it. I sure as hell didn't want everyone knowing about it. They do now, don't they? The whole club knows I grew up in that place."

His hand moved from my face to stroke down my arm. "Not many know, but I'm sure they will soon enough. Nothing spreads quite like gossip in a motorcycle club, babe. But no one is going to think less of you for it. If anything, they'll think more of you for escaping and getting free." He paused and cleared his throat, making me nervous about what he was going to say next. "Missy, I need to know what they did to you last night."

I looked up into his gaze again. "You saw what they did. My stepfather got his men to hold me down so he could strip and beat me."

When he narrowed his eyes, it became clear what he wanted to know. "They didn't rape me. I'm sure they intended to, but you got there in time." I paused to chew my lower lip for a moment. "What made you come when you did, Tiny?"

I'd been sure he'd either not noticed I'd gone, or hadn't cared that I'd left. Either way it had hurt deeply that the man who held my heart cared so little.

"I came as soon as I knew you were gone."

That had me scoffing. "I was gone for nearly a week

before you came for me. Try again."

"Monday morning, I didn't know what to say to you. Since I was due to leave on a run only a couple hours after you left, I figured I'd go and clear my head. Work out what the fuck I should do about you while I was on the road. We rolled back in last night, but I still had no fucking idea what to say to you, and I sure as fuck didn't want to see you with any of my brothers. So I avoided the whore room all together, and the entire clubhouse by heading to Styxx. Keg went to the clubhouse after the run, and when Fawn told him that you'd gone, he came and found me to kick my ass for running you off. As soon as I found out, I went to Scout, and he pulled Keys in to track you down."

Frustrated, I lightly banged my forehead against his chest a couple of times. "You are the most confusing man I've ever met. I can't figure out what you want from me. What am I supposed to do now? Am I supposed to go back into the whore room as though nothing happened?"

The growl vibrated through his chest before the sound hit my ears.

"You're no one's whore, Mercedes. You're mine, my old lady."

I jerked away from him in shock. That he knew my real name and that he would choose a club whore for his old lady. "But that's not allowed. And you told me—"

He rolled us over, so I was lying on my back with him looming over me, stealing my breath with how beautiful and commanding he looked.

"I was polluted as fuck Sunday night. And hung over as hell Monday morning. I can't even remember all that I said, but the reason I got so drunk in the first damn place was because I couldn't stand seeing you with those two Cowboys. Watching them fuck you, you enjoying it. It did my head in. From the moment I first saw you six months ago, you were mine. I was just too fucking stupid to accept it."

My mind, and heart, were reeling. He'd just said what I'd always wanted him to say.

"Am I dreaming?"

He barked out a laugh and lowered his face to mine, his beard tickling my skin a moment before his lips pressed against mine. Heat rushed through me, heating me up from the inside out. With a moan I lifted my hands to run my fingers through his hair. My bruised stomach let out a protest, but I ignored it to focus on Tiny. His tongue licked over my lower lip, before I opened to him so he could thrust it in to dance with mine. My muscles relaxed as his scent and taste filled my senses. As the ache in my chest eased, I realized with a shocking clarity that I'd come home. This man above me was my center and always would be. That he actually wanted me back was more than I'd ever hoped for.

Breaking the kiss, he reached down to grab the bottom of the shirt I wore. It was one of his, so the thing was huge on me, and he easily pulled it over my head and off.

"So fucking pretty, babe."

My cheeks heated as I blushed under his praise.

Which was insane, given my experience, yet this man made me feel like a teenager with her first crush. His thumb brushed over my cheek.

"Love that I can make you blush. So fucking sweet."

Before I could think of something to say, he lowered his mouth to mine and kissed me again. His palm covered my breast and he played as he devoured my mouth. By the time he moved his lips down my throat, I was panting and my pussy was throbbing for some attention. I groaned when his beard scraped over my sensitive nipple before the wet heat of his mouth covered the tender bud.

I wrapped my fingers in his hair and held him to me as he switched to my other breast to give it equal treatment.

"Please..."

I needed him inside of me, his cock filling me up and taking me. I *ached* to feel him within me.

"Some patience, babe. I'll do you right."

I tried to tug his hair to get him to move were I wanted him, but he was so much larger and stronger than me. He kissed his way down my torso, skirting around the large bruise on my tummy, as though I wasn't trying to pull him up over me. When I realized what he planned on doing, my breath caught, and when he stroked his tongue over me for the first time, I released my hold on him to throw my hands out to grip the bedding as my back bowed. Pleasure sparked through my blood and I closed my eyes as Tiny covered my core with his mouth and set about devouring me.

Within moments he had me shuddering. For all my sexual experience, I'd never had a man go down on me. I'd given plenty of blow jobs to men since I'd been trained for it back as a young teenager, but none of the men in the commune had given a shit about whether the women who serviced them got off. Same here at the club. For the most part, they made sure I came when we fucked, but they'd never put their mouths on me like this.

Planting my feet flat on the bed, I rocked my hips against his face as he thrust his tongue in deep. On the third thrust into me, he flicked his thumb over my clit and I came apart, my channel clenching as I cried out his name. I vaguely heard him growl out my name, then somehow he got his jeans off and was up over me in moments. A grin spread over my face when he slid his cock in deep. Tender from my climax, I felt every inch of him as he penetrated me in one, smooth stroke. From the first time I'd had sex with Tiny, I'd loved how he filled me up completely. He was larger than any other lover I'd ever taken and it was as though I'd been built just for him, the perfect size to fit his length and width.

Chapter 5

Tiny

Being balls deep inside my woman was heaven. I knew I'd never get tired of loving on her. *My old lady.* The tingling down my spine told me I didn't have long before I'd come but I wasn't ready to stop. She was slick with sweat and writhing under me as I thrust in and out of her heat. Running a hand down her thigh, I lifted it up until her leg was up against my torso, her foot over my shoulder. The angle opened her up more and allowed me to get inside her deeper. When my cockhead tapped her cervix I winced, expecting her to curse at the pain, but she shuddered and groaned a happy sound. So I did it again, careful not to be too rough. Being as big as I was, this wasn't the first time I'd bottomed out in a woman, and over the years I'd learned how to best play a woman's body.

It wasn't long before her body was shaking on the verge of another climax, and when her channel rippled around me, I couldn't hold back. Dropping her leg down around my waist, I pounded into her as I filled her with my come. She cried out and clenched down on me as she followed me over the edge.

"Fuck me."

When the storm had passed I dropped down over her, giving her my weight for a few moments before rolling to the side so I could gather her up against me. She was so fucking small against me, but she wasn't weak. Nope, my girl was strong as forged steel, and she could more than handle me and the life of being an old lady. Not every woman would be able to cut it as an old lady, and I'd seen plenty of brothers choose wrong. That was what I'd been worried about, but I'd been wrong. I needed to focus on my brothers who'd chosen right. The ones who'd picked women like Missy, who were built for this kind of life.

After growing up in that commune, she craved the safety of being in with a group like the Charon MC. I could see clearly now that she needed it to thrive. And even though she'd been one of the club whores for the past six months, I knew she'd fit right in with the other old ladies. It helped that she'd never broken the rules. Never threw shit at any of the old ladies, or went after the married brothers. Once the news of how she'd been brought up spread, they'd all understand why she chose to join the club the way she did. It might take a few months for things to settle down, but they would, then she'd find herself with a solid family that would have her back forever.

Her soft, smooth, fingertips traced over my face

before she scraped her nails through my beard.

"I love how this feels against my skin. Don't ever get rid of it."

I smiled and turned to catch a finger between my lips so I could nip the end.

"You giving me orders already, woman?"

I'd meant it as a joke, but her skin paled as her eyes widened. *Fuck.* She tried to pull away but I held her tight.

"I was joking, babe. You can give me all the orders you want. Can't promise I'll deliver on all of them, but my beard is definitely here to stay so I'm glad you like it."

The tension left her muscles and she relaxed back against me.

"What happened to them last night?"

As much as I'd been waiting for her to ask, I didn't want to tell her they were here in the same building.

"You don't need to ever worry about them again, Missy."

"So they're dead?"

She'd gone wide-eyed again, but I wasn't sure why exactly. Is that what she wanted to hear? That they were all dead.

"No, baby, they're not dead. They're roughed up, but as far as I know they're all still breathing. Keys has some big plan for them, although I'm not sure what it is. I left them to it, to take care of you."

She chewed her lower lip for a moment. "Do you think I could see him? My stepfather."

That had me jerking back. "What the fuck for?"

She shrugged a shoulder. "Closure, I guess. I have some things I need to say to him so I can close that part of my life and move forward with a clear mind."

I sensed it was more than that, but hell, what could it hurt? The bastard was chained up down in the basement and couldn't physically hurt her. If he tried to verbally, I'd soon shut him up.

"Let me run it by Scout, see what we can do."

Not wanting to leave her, I rolled over to grab my phone from the bedside table without leaving the bed, then dialed. Scout picked up on the second ring.

"Hey, Tiny, didn't expect to hear from you for hours yet. Something wrong?"

"Nothing's wrong. Missy's just wondering if she can have a couple minutes with her stepfather. Wants to tell him something, apparently."

Scout's laugh was dark. "Sure, she wants to *speak* with him. Make sure you show her how to throw a punch before you let her in there. Don't need her busting up her hands on the fucker. Taz has been down with him for a few hours now, so not sure how much longer he's got in him."

I frowned at that. "I thought you wanted them alive?"

"We did. And hopefully once Taz finishes his thing we'll have what we need and it won't matter if he dies or not."

"You gonna tell me what exactly Keys has planned?"

"Sure, but not right now. Get your girl cleaned up and

down here. I'll go see if Taz is ready for a break."

I hung up after Scout cut the line, but wasn't sure what to make of what the fuck they were doing with the assholes we'd picked up.

"So, what's going on?"

I glanced over at Missy and smiled. Such a pretty little thing, with her sex-messed hair and reddened lips from all the attention I'd given her. And she was all fucking mine.

"You'll get your wish. Taz has been in with him, so not sure on the condition he'll be in."

With a nod, she scooted over to the edge of mattress and rose to stand, before she stalled out.

"Um, I don't suppose someone picked up my bag last night?"

I stood from the bed and went over to the closet to retrieve it for her. "Sure did. Here you go."

She gave me a coy smile. "You gonna come help scrub my back for me?"

With a chuckle, I shook my head. "I do that, we won't be leaving this room for another couple hours, babe."

Giggling, she strode into the bathroom, twitching her ass at me the whole way. Damn woman was trying to drive me fucking crazy. Turning away from the temptation of her hot little body, I gave her five minutes before I grabbed a change of clothes for myself and followed her into the bathroom. I needed to clean up before we went downstairs. My beard was a fucking mess after me going down on her. I grinned, and decided it was totally worth the few extra minutes it was gonna take me to get ready in the mornings to wake up like that on the regular.

I slipped into the shower behind her and pressed a kiss to her wet shoulder.

"I thought we didn't have time for water sports today?"

"We don't, but I need to clean up and wash out my beard before we go downstairs."

The red that bloomed over her face had me grinning. Totally loved how, despite her experience, I could make her blush so easily.

"Ah, yeah. I'll leave you to it then."

She slid out of the shower and I got a nice show watching her dry off and dress as I washed. Once she left the bathroom, I focused on what I was doing, and made fast work of getting myself clean, dried and dressed. Then we were heading down the hallway toward the stairs. Once we hit the ground floor, I took her hand and led her to Scout's office. Knocking on the door, I walked in and found him sitting behind his desk, not looking happy.

"We good to go down?"

"Ah, yeah, sure. Fuck, this shit doesn't sit well with me."

With all that was currently going on, I had no idea which part Scout had an issue with. I knew it wasn't the part about keeping Missy safe. "What part?"

"Having to keep those fuckers above ground. Men

like that deserve to be put down, hard."

"Can you just tell me what the fuck is going on? All this cryptic shit is starting to make me twitchy."

He glanced from me to Missy, then back again. "I know this place loves gossip, but if I hear either of you have told this to anyone, it ain't gonna end well, we clear?"

"Crystal, prez."

"I won't say a word."

As Missy spoke I pulled her in against me while Scout went and shut the door before he moved to lean against the front of his desk.

"Taz lost his mother and baby sister to his stepfather." Missy gasped and I was tempted to make a similar noise.

"That's the tats, yeah? Lola and Grace?"

Scout nodded at my comment. "Yep. So naturally, he's taken an interest in this current situation. For him, and us, it's not enough to simply put down these bastards. Not when there's a whole fucking network of them preying on other women. So, we've gotten a friend of the club involved and once Taz finishes his fun and games, they'll all be handed over to the FBI. They've promised us they'll go in and do what they need to do to shut that commune down for good. We'll keep an eye on them, and if they don't step up, we'll step in and take care of it like we normally do."

That had me frowning. "Why aren't we just going in to clean house?"

"Because it ain't that simple. It's not one or two guys

being bastards, but a whole fucking cult. And it's not local. We got no backing there. What the hell do we do with all the innocent women and children? It's a helluva lot easier to let the feds handle it in this situation. No matter how much I want to be the one who's behind these fuckers going down, even I can see it wouldn't be that simple. And I don't want to spend the rest of my life in a fucking jail cell if I don't have to. Got me?"

I nodded. "Yeah, I get it. How long have we had a friend in with the feds?"

"It's new. Someone Taz, Mac and Eagle worked with in their Marine days. I don't intend on working with them often, but like I said. It's the best solution for this situation."

"What's going to happen to them all?"

Missy's voice was quiet, but it got our attention.

"Not real sure, sweetheart. The ones who attacked you are heading for prison, I made sure of that before I agreed to hand them over. And just to make sure they learn their lesson not to fuck with us, Keys found a little something that we can do to them to make sure they have a limited love life for the rest of their days. If you catch my drift."

Damn, my balls shrunk up tight against my body in sympathy. I was certain I didn't want more details on that one.

Missy

"As to the ones still in the commune, that's gonna take them time to figure out. Counseling will be offered to the victims, along with assistance for them to resettle elsewhere. It's not going to be easy, or fast. But charges will be filed where possible, and all the women and kids will gain their freedom. And speaking of freedom..." Scout stood and moved behind his desk where he opened a drawer and pulled an envelope free. "Got these for you in the deal, too. You're now legally here in the US, Missy."

I took the envelope, not really believing what he'd said. Was it even possible? Pulling the documents free, I glanced over each one. Birth certificate, passport... other paperwork. I looked back up to Scout.

"This is all real? Like, fully legit?"

"Well, it did come from the FBI, so I would assume it's all legal and above board. You're truly free now, Missy." He paused. "Or do you want to go by Mercedes now?"

Tears pricked my eyes. I could go anywhere, do anything. No more having to hide in shadows when I was outside the clubhouse. No one could send me back to Mexico, where I didn't know anyone, or anything about how to live there.

"I want to be Mercedes again. I'm my mother's daughter."

My heart ached that I got all this because she'd died to protect me. But I honestly felt she would have approved of my decision to stay here to be with Tiny.

Tiny cleared his throat, the sound a nervous one. "So, now you're free. What are you planning on doing?"

I turned to face him and the look on his face broke my heart. Did he really think I would walk away from him now?

"You crazy man, what do you think I'm going to do? Run off into the sunset? I love you. I know Scout told me at the beginning not to lose my heart to a Charon, but that's what happened. You took possession of my heart long ago. I wouldn't want to be anywhere but right here with you." Then a thought struck me. "Unless you don't want me here? Did you only say I could be your old lady because you thought I was stuck here?"

I tried to move away from him, but with a growl he snatched me back to him, wrapping his big arms around me so I was pinned against his muscular body.

"That's what you think? That I just want you because you're convenient? That's a load of shit, babe. You haven't been convenient since the first time I fucked you. That's all it took, one fucking touch and you had me caught. You've been mine a while now, I was just too fucking stupid to see it. But I won't be like your stepfamily, I won't hold you here if you don't want to be here. You'll take my heart with you if you leave, but I won't stop you."

Tears were streaming down my face as I looked up at Tiny. *My old man.*

"Kiss me?"

With a feral grin, he lifted me up, and pressing my

back against the wall, took my mouth in a hard, passionate kiss. Until Scout clapped his hands with a loud crack.

"I'm all for live porn, but we don't have the time right now. We're gonna be handing over those fuckers tonight so we've got a lot to do with them today. Oh, and, Tiny?"

Tiny lowered me so my feet were back on the floor before he turned back toward Scout.

"Yeah?"

"You might have been slow off the mark, but I'm not. Here's her cut. Mercedes, you wear that whenever you're around the club and you won't get any trouble from anyone. If any of the brothers do try to treat you like you're still one of the whores, you let me know and I'll fucking deal with them."

I wiped my face with the bottom of my shirt before taking a step toward where Tiny was taking a leather vest from Scout. This was all getting very real now. I'd seen the respect the women who wore these cuts got. The Charon brothers were the kings of this place, but the old ladies? They were the queens. I still wasn't certain I was worthy, but if Tiny and Scout both thought I was, who was I to argue? I mean, the president of the club would know who was deserving and who wasn't, right?

Tiny's grin was wide and his eyes looked a little damp as he tugged on my hand to bring me back in close to him. He held the cut out for me, I slid my arms through the holes and when Tiny pulled the front halves closed across my chest, I pressed my nose against the shoulder and inhaled. The leather smell made me think of him and my blood heated with arousal.

"*Property of Tiny*. Has a nice ring to it. Now, let's get downstairs before I forget all about you wanting a word with that piece of shit, and take you back upstairs like I want to."

Leaning in, I pressed a kiss over his heart. "Soon, babe. Just give me five minutes with him. Then I'm all yours."

"Damn straight you are. All mine, for always."

Scout made a gagging noise and shoved us out of his office, which had us both chuckling until we got to the hidden stairs toward the rear of the building. As Tiny opened the way, all levity disappeared. Taking my hand, he silently led me down a flight of stairs I'd never realized were there.

When we reached a thick timber door, Tiny reached up and pounded on it three times. A moment later, Taz opened the way and stepped out into the hallway. He was shirtless and was wiping blood from his hands with a rag.

"Hey, Missy. Cut looks good on you. You want a minute or two with him?"

"Ah, yeah, and I'm going to go by my real name now. Mercedes."

Taz gave me a nod. "Good deal. Mercedes it is. Do whatever you want to him. Pretty sure he's told me all he has to tell me. If you take it too far, it's no skin off my nose."

I frowned, unsure whether to voice my question, as I

didn't know if we were supposed to know what Scout had just told us. Tiny cut my thoughts off when he asked what I was thinking.

"Won't your friends be pissed with that?"

Taz smirked. "Probably, but they're getting so many new toys. One less won't bother them too much. But, if you do want to get messy with him, take your cut off, luv. Don't want to get his dirty blood on it."

I nodded. "I want him to see me in it first. Thanks, Taz."

As I moved to go into the room, the light caught on Taz's chest highlighting the words tattooed in large letters over his pecs. Lola and Grace. My heart ached for Taz, to have lost both a mother and sister. I couldn't imagine. I opened my mouth but one look at his face had me closing it before I uttered a word. With my chin held high, I strode into the room, Tiny and Taz following me in before the door was closed.

The smell of blood and other things was so strong in the air, it had me clearing my throat a few times.

"Yeah, the smell's pretty bad. Sorry about that."

A groan had me looking to the back of the cell and cringing. Damn, Taz had been busy. With a deep breath, I tilted my chin up a notch and strode over to stand right in front of my stepfather.

"Hello, Gerald."

He curled his lip as hatred burned in his eyes. I'd never called him by his name before, he'd always insisted I call him stepfather.

"What do you want?"

His words were slightly slurred, like he couldn't quite move his jaw normally.

"His jaw is a little fucked up. Might be a little tricky to hear him. Not that he has anything to say that's worth hearing."

I'd never heard Taz speak with such hatred, but then, I knew full well how Gerald could bring that emotion out in a person.

"That's okay. I mainly just wanted to see him broken like this. To replace the image in my head of him lording over me with one of him as he truly is. Nothing but a weak, pathetic bastard who thought hurting those weaker than him was the only way he could gain any power."

He growled a low rumble, sounding almost animalistic.

"I have no idea why my mother stayed with you for so long. She deserved so much better."

"It's your fault she stayed. To save you, she whored herself out to whoever, whatever I wanted from her."

A shot of pain flashed through me at his words, which he'd managed to say clearer than before. It was nothing my mother hadn't confessed to me before she died.

I shook my head. "No. That wasn't on me. That was on you. You and your asshole buddies who would threaten a mother with the well-being of her child to get what you wanted from her. Did she even know what I was being trained for at that school? That you always intended to treat me just like her in the end?"

He grinned. Well, I assumed he was attempting to grin. Taz had really done a good job on his face. It was a mess.

"She had no idea you were being trained. She thought she was taking your place when I brought others around. You illegal immigrants make the best slaves. So willing to do anything to stay in the US. Just wait till I tell those feds about your status. You'll be on the first bus back to Mexico. Then all that training will come in real handy, I'm sure."

I could feel the anger radiating off both Tiny and Taz behind me, but I kept my expression blank as I glanced at the table beside us. At all the blood-covered things laying there. Then I turned to Taz.

"I need to hurt him, do some damage he won't forget. What do you suggest?"

The feral grin that spread over Taz's face would have scared the fuck out of me if I didn't know the man. But before he'd taken Flick for his old lady, he'd been a regular in the whore room and he'd always been sweet with us. I knew this harsh, violent side of him was all for Gerald.

"I think you deserve to be the one to end him, luv. Knife to the stomach will do it nice and slow. We'll leave him down here to die slowly. Let him really think over his sins before he goes to hell for them."

My stomach turned. For all my anger at the man, I couldn't do that to him. I shook my head. "No, I can't do that. I know he deserves it, but I just, can't make myself be that cruel. But I would like to be the one to end him. Jail is too good for him, and I don't want to worry about the day he gets released and comes for me. Or my kids."

Yes. That's what this was really for. To keep my and Tiny's kids safe from this monster ever coming for them. I turned to face Tiny and saw the love shining in his eyes.

"Hand me your cut, babe. Taz is right. We don't want to taint that with his filth."

I shrugged out of the leather and handed it to him. Tilting my head up, I waited for him to give me a quick kiss before I released him and turned back to face Gerald for the last time.

Taz handed me a huge, nasty looking knife, and once I took hold of the grip, he wrapped his hand around mine. "Straight through the heart will do it fast. But let me help you get it done. You haven't done this kinda shit before, and we want to get it right first go. Any last words for him?"

I calmly raised my gaze to Gerald's. His eyes were peeled wide now, like he finally understood this shit wasn't going to end well for him.

"I just received all my paperwork, I'm now legally in the US. And now that I've found my home here, I am never leaving it. Not for anyone, especially not for a slimy bastard like you. This is for my mother, and the years you stole from us both."

I lifted my hand, and with Taz's guidance, pressed the tip of the knife against the left side of his chest. I paused to look him straight in the eye.

"Go straight to hell and stay there, asshole."

Then I pushed forward, and Taz added his strength to get the blade in deep enough to enter his heart. I stood there until his eyes went dim and his body limp. Then I released the knife, leaving it embedded in his chest before I turned and strode out of the room. With Tiny by my side, I left my past behind with Gerald's dead body.

Epilogue

One month later
Tiny

"Where are you taking me?"

I glanced over at my woman. *My old lady*. She was wearing tight jeans and a cute off-the-shoulder long sleeve top. Despite it being winter, today was fairly warm so she hadn't added her coat. But she had put on her cut. Fuck, nothing got me hot faster than seeing her wearing my property patch. Oh, and she was also wearing a blindfold. I grinned.

"You'll see soon enough."

This was her first Christmas. Ever. They hadn't celebrated it in the commune. So I was feeling the pressure to get this shit right. I figured I was off to a good start with the present I had waiting for her. Because I wanted to surprise her fully, I'd brought one of the club's cages rather than my bike. I wanted to see her expression when I lifted that blindfold. No way would it have stayed in place if she was behind me on my bike. Nor was it real safe to have her sightless on the back of a Harley.

As I hopped out, I waved at the peanut gallery we had on the opposite sidewalk. Eagle, Silk and their son, Raven, Mac, Zara and their daughter, Cleo, along with Taz and Flick, who was pregnant with their first child. With a wink, I opened Mercedes' door and helped her out to stand in front of our new place.

Standing beside her, I leaned down to whisper to her as I lifted the blindfold.

"Merry Christmas, babe."

The material fell away and my girl's eyes peeled wide as she made that adorable squeaking sound I fucking loved.

"You got us a house?"

She threw herself at me, and with a laugh, I caught her in my arms and held her tight against me.

"Yeah, babe. We need a place of our own. Can't stay in that tiny room at the clubhouse forever. And take a look across the street."

She pulled back to peek over my arm and her grin widened. As I'd predicted, it hadn't taken long for Mercedes to fit in with the other old ladies. A few of the older ones still gave her the cold shoulder, but that was their problem. Silk, Zara and Flick had been all over welcoming her into the fold of the old ladies. Especially once Scout got her a job at Marie's Cafe working with Zara, and when they heard about me buying this place across the street from where they all had their homes.

"We're turning this road into Charon Lane, babe. I'm the fifth Charon to buy down here."

She turned her face up to me on that. "Don't you mean the fourth?"

I smirked and tapped the tip of her nose with my forefinger. "Nope, fifth. We just settled fourth. And no, I ain't telling you who. It'll be another surprise for you to enjoy when it happens."

"Kiss me, then show me our house."

I loved how she demanded I kiss her. She'd told me because she was so damn short, she couldn't just kiss me, unless I was sitting down. So she just asked, well, it was more like a demand, for what she wanted. And I always delivered.

"I love you so much, Mercedes, and I can't wait to turn this house into a home with you."

"And I love you, Ryan Nelson. And all I need to be home is to be with you."

I grinned at the smug look on her face. She loved that she was the only one who ever used my real name. I lowered my mouth to hers and stopped her talking with the kiss she'd wanted. One of the guys across the road wolf-whistled and I flipped him the bird without looking at them, as I kept on kissing my woman. I'd been such a fool to be afraid of settling down. Having Mercedes in my life, always there to come home to, made everything in my world brighter, lighter. Made life worth living.

Life was good.

Other Charon MC Books:

Book 1:

Inking Eagle

***The sins of her father will be her undoing... unless a
hero rides to her rescue.***

As the 15th anniversary of the 9/11 attacks nears, Silk
struggles to avoid all reminders of the day she was
orphaned. She's working hard in her tattoo shop, Silky
Ink, and working even harder to keep her eyes and her
hands off her bodyguard, Eagle. She'd love to forget her
sorrows in his strong arms.

But Eagle is a prospect in the Charon MC, and her
uncle is the VP. As a Daughter of the Club, she's off
limits to the former Marine. But not for long. As soon as
he patches in, he intends to claim Silk for his old lady.
He'll wear her ink, and she'll wear his patch.

Too late, they learn that Silk's father had dark secrets, ones that have lived beyond his grave. When demons from the past come for Silk, Eagle will need all the skills he learned in the Marines to get his woman back safe, and keep her that way.

For more information and buy links visit:

http://khloewren.com/InkingEagle.html

Book 2:

Fighting Mac

*She's no sleeping beauty, but then he's no prince -
just a biker warrior to the rescue.*

For the past three years Claire 'Zara' Flynn has been at
the mercy of narcolepsy and cataplexy attacks. But after
she witnesses a shooting by the ruthless Iron Hammers
MC, her problems get a whole lot worse. She's now a
marked woman, on the run for her life.

Former Marine Jacob 'Mac' Miller has a good life with
the Charon MC. He works in the club gym and teaches
self-defense classes - in the hopes of saving other women
from the violent death his sister suffered. When the
pretty new waitress at a local cafe catches his attention,
he wants her in his bed. But there's a problem. She's
clearly scared of all bikers. Wanting to help her, he talks
her into coming to his class. Mac soon realizes he wants
to keep her close in more ways than one. But can he,
when his club's worst enemies come after her?

When Zara disappears, Mac and his brothers must go to war to get her back. Because this time, she wakes up in a terrible place... surrounded by other desperate women, and guarded by the Iron Hammers MC. Can her leather-clad prince ride to the rescue in time to save her from hell?

For more information and buy links visit:

http://khloewren.com/FightingMac.html

Book 3:

Chasing Taz

He lived his life one conquest at a time. She calculated her every move… until she met him.

Former Marine Donovan 'Taz' Lee might appear to be a carefree Aussie bloke living it up as a member of the Texan motorcycle club, Charon MC, but the truth is so much more complicated. With blood and tears haunting his past and threatening to destroy his future, Taz is completely unprepared for the woman of his dreams, when she comes in and knocks him on his ass. Literally.

Felicity "Flick" Vaughn joined the FBI to get answers behind her brother's dishonorable discharge and abandonment of his family. Knowing Taz was a part of her brother's final mission, she agrees to partner with him to go after a bigger club, The Satan's Cowboys MC.

However, nothing in life is ever simple and Flick is totally unprepared to have genuine feelings for the sexy Aussie. When secrets are revealed and their worlds are busted wide open, will they be strong enough to still be standing when the dust settles?

For more information and buy links visit:

http://khloewren.com/ChasingTaz.html